THE HARE and the TORTOISE

Retold & Illustrated by

HELEN WARD

Urdu translation by Qamar Zamani

mantra

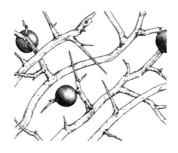

To tortoises everywhere

First published in Great Britain in 1998 by The Templar Company plc
First dual language publication in 2005 by Mantra Lingua
by arrangement with The Templar Company plc
Copyright © 1998 by The Templar Company plc
Dual language copyright © 2005 by Mantra Lingua

Edited by AJ Wood
Additional design by Mike Jolley

This book was drawn in ink and painted
in watercolour and gouache on watercolour paper.

Mantra Lingua
Global House, 303 Ballards Lane, London N12 8NP
www.mantralingua.com

ایک زمانے میں ایک بہت تیز رفتار خرگوش اور ایک بے حد سست رفتار کچھوا رہتے تھے۔

There once was a very fast hare and a very slow tortoise.

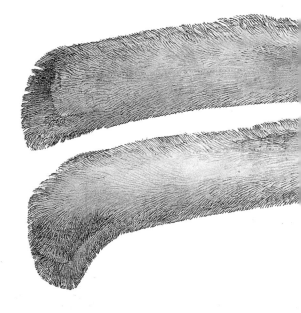

The hare hurtled everywhere causing havoc.

خرگوش اپنی گود پھاند سے ہر طرف تباہی مچاتا رہتا تھا۔

کچھوا ایک نہایت سست اور خیالوں میں ڈوبا رہنے والا جانور تھا۔

The tortoise
was an altogether slower and
more thoughtful animal.

ایک دن خرگوش سرپٹ بھاگا جا رہا تھا کہ اُس کی کچھوے سے ٹھوکر لگ گئی اور وہ لڑھکتا ہوا ایک کانٹوں بھری جھاڑی میں گر گیا۔۔۔ خوب تکلیف ہوئی۔

One day, the hare was sprinting along when he tripped over the tortoise and tumbled into a thorny bush… which hurt.

خرگوش نے کچھوے پر چیخنا چلانا شروع کر دیا۔ اُس نے کچھوے کو کاہل اور بیوقوف کہا۔ یہ شور سُن کر ایک بھیڑ جمع ہو گئی۔ کچھوے نے خرگوش سے یہ تو نہیں کہا کہ اُس کی اپنی رائے خرگوش کے متعلق کیا تھی۔ بلکہ اُس کو ایک دوڑ کا مقابلہ کرنے کی دعوت دی۔

The hare shouted at the tortoise.
He called the tortoise slow and stupid. The noise attracted a crowd.
The tortoise did not say what he thought of the hare. Instead, he challenged him to a race.

خرگوش ہنسی سے بے حال ہو گیا یہاں تک کہ اُس کے زخموں میں اور زیادہ تکلیف ہونے لگی۔

The hare laughed so much that he hurt even more.

اِس مقابلے کی خبر چاروں طرف پھیل گئی اور جانور دنیا کے ہر کونے سے آنے لگے۔

دوڑ کا راستہ مقرر کر دیا گیا۔۔۔

News of the challenge spread and the animals came from all corners of the earth.
The course was marked out…

and a referee was found.

اور ایک نگران بھی تلاش کر لیا گیا۔

آخرکار وہ اہم دن آ پہنچا!
نگران نے آواز لگائی۔ ''اپنی جگہ لو۔۔۔ تیاری کرو۔۔۔ بھاگو!''
خرگوش چھلانگیں لگاتا ہوا تیر کی طرح بھاگا اور نظروں سے غائب ہو گیا۔

At last the great day arrived!
The referee shouted:
"On your marks… get set… GO!"
The hare hurtled forward
in a leap and a bound
and was gone.

کچھوا آہستہ آہستہ ایک ہی رفتار سے رینگتا ہوا، ایک کے بعد دوسرا پیر رکھتا ہوا، پیچھے ہی رہ گیا۔

The tortoise slowly and steadily plodded along, one foot after the other, and was soon left behind.

خرگوش نے دریا تک دوڑ لگائی اور چھلانگیں لگاتا ہوا۔۔۔

The hare raced to
the river
and leaped…

ایک پتھر سے دوسرے پتھر تک۔۔۔

from stone… to stone…

اگلے کنارے تک پہنچ گیا۔۔۔

towards the far bank…

لیکن اپنے خیال میں اُس کو جہاں جانا تھا دراصل وہ اُس جگہ نہیں پہنچا۔

but he did not quite get to where he thought he was going.

The tortoise crossed more easily.

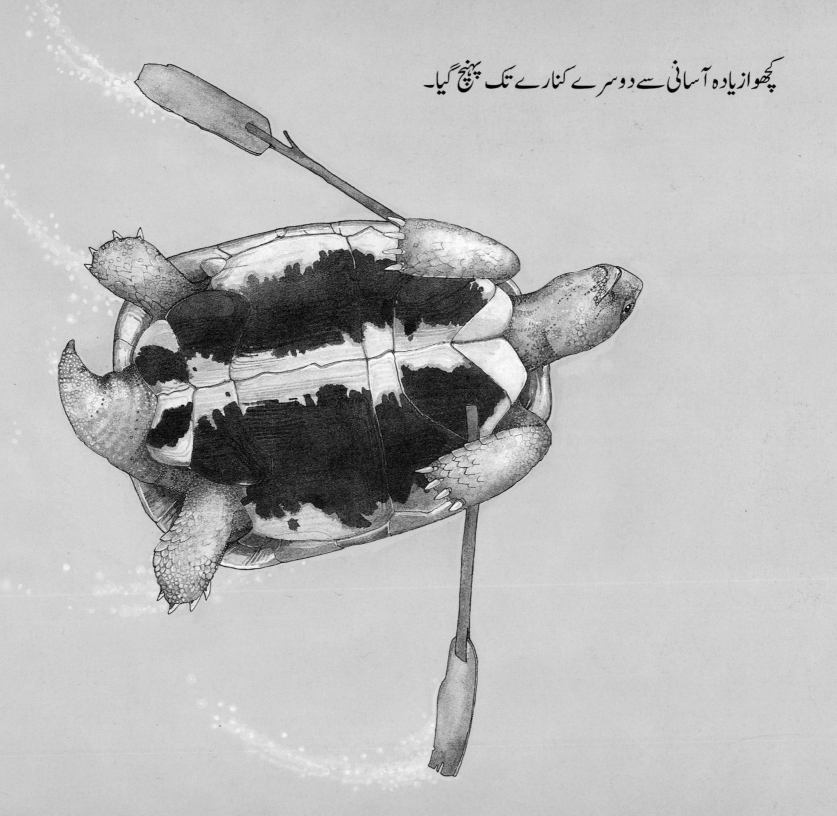

کچھوا زیادہ آسانی سے دوسرے کنارے تک پہنچ گیا۔

Next, the hare found himself in the thick of a very peculiar forest.

پھر کیا ہوا خرگوش نے اپنے آپ کو ایک نہایت عجیب و غریب جنگل میں پایا۔

خرگوش کے جسم میں کھونچیں لگی ہوئی تھیں اور
وہ اِس قدر تھکا ہوا تھا کہ دوسرے کنارے پر
پہنچ کر اُس نے فیصلہ کیا کہ کچھ دیر نیند کی جھپکی لے لے۔۔۔

The hare was scratched and so tired
when he reached the other side
that he decided to take a nap…

یہ تو ظاہر تھا کہ کچھوے کو اُن درختوں کے درمیان بھٹکتے اور لڑھکتے ہوئے یہاں پہنچنے میں بہت دیر لگ جائے گی۔۔۔

After all, it was going to take the tortoise
a very long time indeed to scramble
through those trees...

جب خرگوش نیند سے جاگا تو اُس نے چاروں طرف نظر دوڑائی۔

The hare woke up
and looked
around.

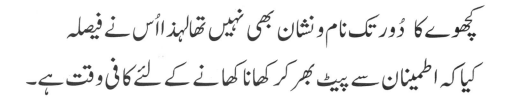

کچھوے کا دُور تک نام و نشان بھی نہیں تھا لہٰذا اُس نے فیصلہ کیا کہ اطمینان سے پیٹ بھر کر کھانا کھانے کے لئے کافی وقت ہے۔

He could not see the tortoise anywhere.
So the hare decided that he had enough time for a long lunch.

Or so he thought...

کم از کم اُس کا یہی خیال تھا۔۔۔

خرگوش کھانا تقریباً ختم ہی کر چکا تھا جب اُس کو خوشی کے نعرے لگانے کی آواز آئی۔

The hare had nearly eaten
everything when he was
surprised to hear
the sound of cheering.

سخت دہشت کے عالم میں، حلق تک بھرے پیٹ کے ساتھ ،
خرگوش جتنی تیز رفتاری سے دوڑ سکتا تھا ، دوڑا۔

Horrified, he ran as fast as a hare
with a large lunch inside him could run.

لیکن یہ تیز رفتاری کافی نہیں تھی! صبر سے کام لینے والا، سست رفتاری سے رینگتا ہوا کچھوا اِس سے پہلے ہی جیت کے مقام تک پہنچ چکا تھا۔ حالانکہ خرگوش کی تیز رفتاری دوڑ جیتنے کے لئے تو کافی نہیں تھی۔

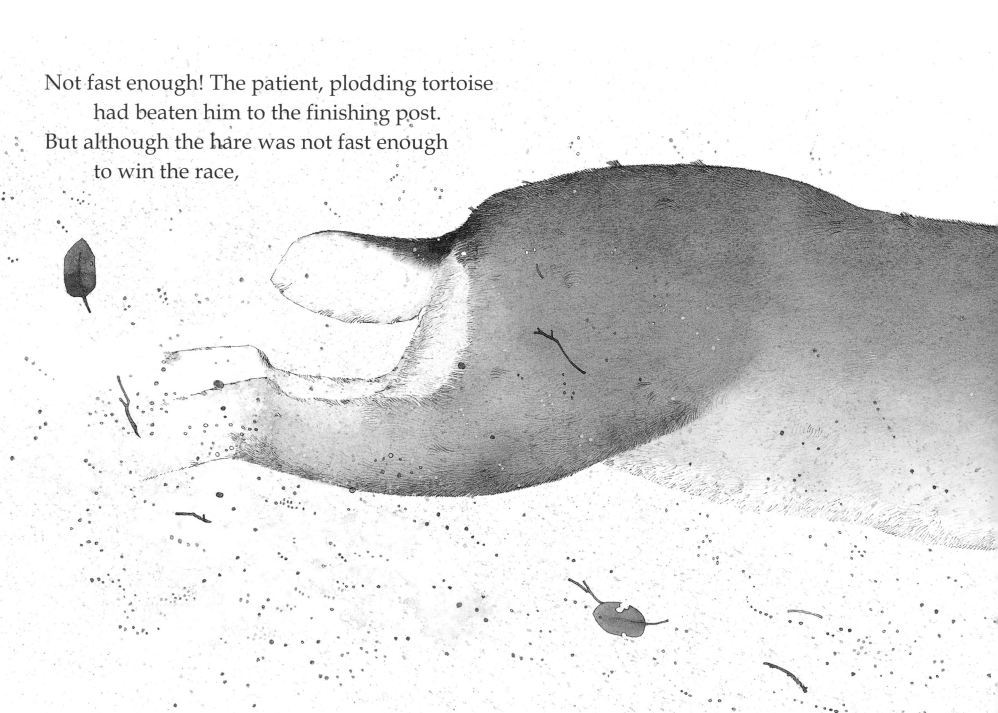

Not fast enough! The patient, plodding tortoise
    had beaten him to the finishing post.
But although the hare was not fast enough
    to win the race,

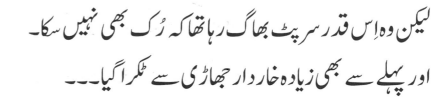

لیکن وہ اِس قدر سرپٹ بھاگ رہا تھا کہ رُک بھی نہیں سکا۔
اور پہلے سے بھی زیادہ خاردار جھاڑی سے ٹکرا گیا۔۔۔

he was running too fast to stop.
He crashed into an even thornier bush than before…

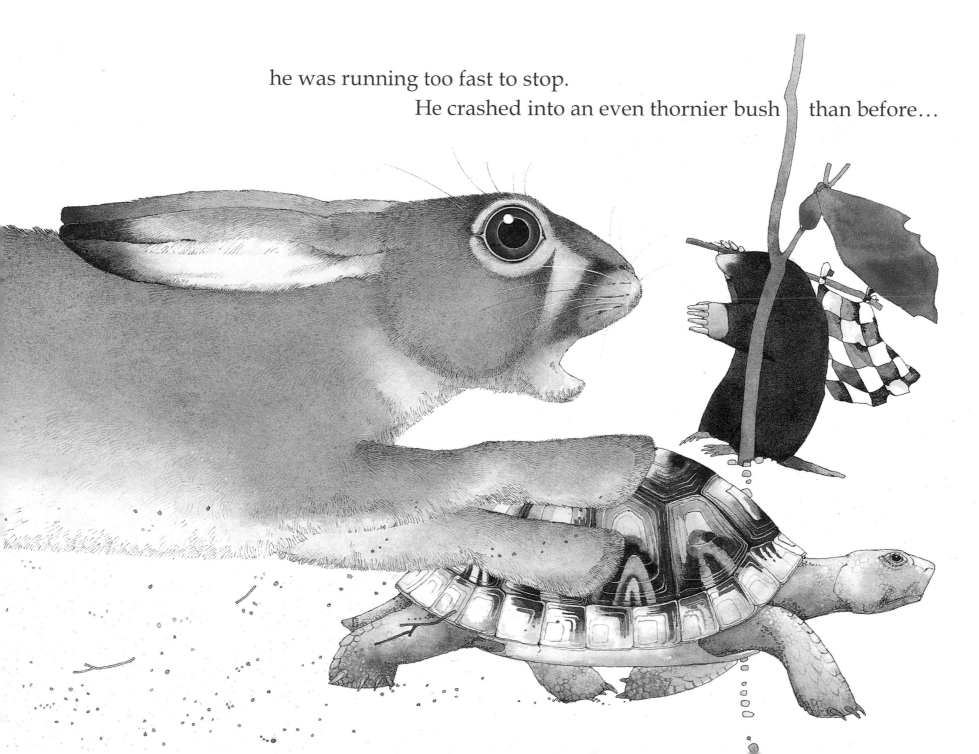

لیکن اِس مرتبہ وہ کچھ نہیں بولا۔

But this time
he said nothing.

OTHER ANIMALS

There Was Once a Very Fast Hare...

All species of hare are fast runners, thanks to their long hind legs and strong leg muscles. The common brown hare *(Lepus capensis)*, illustrated throughout this book, is found in many parts of the world. It was introduced into the Americas, Australia and New Zealand from its original home in Europe so that it could be hunted for food and sport. Unlike many other small mammals, it does not burrow, but relies on its speed and vigilance to escape danger. Just as well, then, that grown male hares can reach speeds of up to 70kms per hour - faster than the world's fastest racehorse!

...And a Very Slow Tortoise.

Although not the slowest creatures on the planet, tortoises have a long-standing reputation for slowness. Most move at speeds of around only 360m per hour - in other words, it would take 3 hours for our hero to travel a mere 1km! The belief that tortoises hardly move at all is not helped by the fact that, when threatened, they will not try to flee like most other animals. Instead, a frightened tortoise will stay perfectly still, retracting its head and feet beneath its armoured shell, in the hope that this will provide sufficient protection from its enemies. The tortoise painted throughout this book is known as Hermann's tortoise *(Testudo hermanni)*, the species most commonly supplied to the pet trade.

Causing Havoc

None of these creatures is speedy enough to get out of the way of a hurrying hare. In the case of the edible snail, that's hardly surprising since it is one of the slowest creatures on the planet, taking an hour to move only 4.5m. From left to right you can see an ocellated lizard, cockchafer, garden dormouse and quail, as well as the Roman or edible snail.

An Altogether More Thoughtful Animal

How thoughtful of the tortoise to provide this dwarf mongoose with a look-out post! The mongoose is a speedy snake-catcher, often kept as a pet in its original home of Asia.

The Noise Attracted A Crowd

Apart from the hare and the tortoise, the gathering crowd shows, from left to right, the dwarf mongoose, common chameleon, European quail, fennec fox, impala, short-horned grasshopper and a banded snail.

From All Corners of the Earth ... (far left)

Amongst the animals that have gathered from far and wide you can see the world's fastest flying bird, the peregrine falcon. This impressive bird of prey will dive through the sky at speeds reaching 131kms per hour or more, knocking its prey of other smaller birds to the

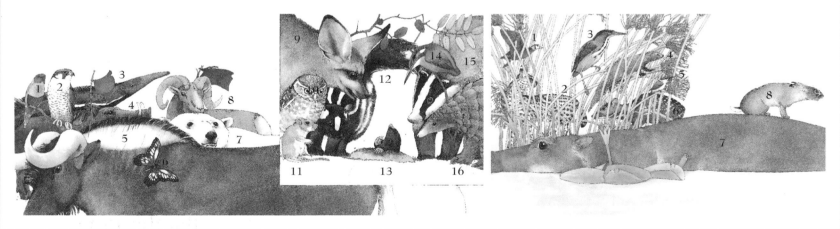

ground with a single blow of its sharp talons! At the opposite end of the scale, you can also see the dusky swallowtail butterfly, possessor of the slowest wingbeat in the insect world at 300 beats per minute!

1. Rainbow lory	2. Peregrine falcon
3. Giant anteater	4. African warthog
5. White-tailed gnu	6. Dusky swallowtail butterfly
7. Polar bear	8. American bighorn sheep
9. Bat-eared fox	10. Burrowing owl
11. African gerbil	12. Spotted skunk
13. European mole	14. Kingfisher
15. Eurasian badger	16. Pangolin

But He Did Not Quite Get
To Where He Thought He Was Going (left)

Like the tortoise, the hippopotamus has a reputation for being slow and lazy. True, hippos do spend practically all day resting but they can actually move quite quickly when they want to, especially when running along the river bottom. However, they are most often found standing up to their necks in river water or reed beds where they can sleep unobserved, with only their eyes and nostrils poking up above the surface.

The group of waterside dwellers also includes:

1. Pygmy goose	2. Serval
3. Green heron	4. Egyptian mongoose
5. Water chevrotain	6. White-collared kingfisher
7. Hippopotamus	8. Hare

A Very Peculiar Forest (above)

Amongst this fine array of legs are those belonging to some of the speediest creatures on earth.

The cheetah is the fastest mammal on land and can reach speeds of over 100kms per hour when chasing its prey across the African plains. It shares its home with the world's fastest land bird - the ostrich. With its powerful legs, flexible knees and two-toed feet, the ostrich is capable of reaching 72kms per hour - fast enough to outrun most of its enemies, which is just as well since it is too big to fly! Most of the other animals shown are also quick on their feet apart, of course, from the slow loris who, as its name implies, spends most of its life climbing slowly through the branches of its forest home.

1. Thomson's gazelle	2. Slow loris
3. Hare	4. Ostrich
5. Cheetah	6. Oryx
7. Indian rhinoceros	8. African elephant
9. Giraffe	10. Vicuna
11. Common ringtail	12. Red river hog
13. Okapi	

When He Reached The Other Side (above)

Continuing through the forest of legs you can see:

1. Pronghorn antelope
2. Giant elephant shrew
3. Bongo
4. Giraffe
5. Gouldian finch
6. De Brazza's monkey
7. Zebra
8. Emu
9. And, of course, a very tired hare!

Plenty Of Time For A Long Lunch...

Did you spot the chinchilla (top) and northern grasshopper mouse (bottom) hiding amongst the vegetables? Both are used to living in the most inhospitable climates - the grasshopper mouse in the hot, dry deserts of North America, the chinchilla in the cold, rocky mountains of Bolivia and Chile.

The Sound Of Cheering (right)

And so we reach the end of the race! You might have expected the cheetah to have got there before the hare - after all, he is the fastest creature on earth, but somehow even the world's slowest animals have managed to make it to the finishing post as well! The three-toed sloth holds the record for being the slowest mammal, crawling along on the ground at a mere 158m per hour.

It would take the sloth over 6 hours to travel 1km. In fact, this animal spends so much time staying still that microscopic algae actually grow on its fur. However, even the sloth is faster than the red slug who would take over 3 weeks to travel that same kilometre!

1. Roadrunner - takes third place as the fastest land bird after the ostrich and emu, running at 42kms per hour.
2. Armadillo - although capable of moving quite quickly the nine-banded armadillo holds the record for being one of the sleepiest animals on earth, spending 80% of its life fast asleep, not moving at all!
3. Cheetah - the fastest land mammal at 115kms per hour.
4. Tern - holds the record for the longest flight of any bird at 26,000kms.
5. Blackbuck - third fastest land mammal after the cheetah and pronghorn antelope, running at 80kms per hour.
6. Camel - at 16kms per hour, the camel is one of the fastest large animals in the desert.

7. Long-tailed hummingbird - hummingbirds have the fastest wingbeats in the bird world, reaching 90 beats a second in some species.
8. European mole - a champion digger, the mole can dig over 20m in a single day.
9. Giraffe - possessor of the longest legs in the animal kingdom, the giraffe can run at 50kms per hour.
10. Monarch butterfly - makes the longest journey of any insect at 3,432kms.
11. Kangaroo - this marsupial can jump almost 4m in a single giant leap and reach a speed of 45kms per hour.
12. Banded snail - Although faster than the edible snail, the banded variety would still take over a week to travel a single kilometre!
13. Three-toed sloth - the world's slowest mammal, moving at only 158m per hour.
14. Gentoo penguin - the fastest swimmer in the bird world, with a top speed of 27kms per hour.
15. Red slug - the world's slowest creature at 1.8m per hour.
16. And, to finish, who else but the slow and steady Hermann's tortoise!